Rosie and Sarah ran toward the sound of the clanging fire engine bells. As they turned the corner, three large white horses pulling a red fire wagon with hoses thundered past them. Followed by another. And another one loaded with ladders.

"Must be a big fire," said Sarah.

People were running down the street after the wagons. Rosie and Sarah stopped an old woman with a kerchief on her head, still wearing her apron.

"Have you heard?" Rosie asked her. "Where's the fire?"

"Washington Square," the woman answered.

They looked up over the buildings toward the square. In the distance, a pillar of black smoke rose into the sky.

"Freyda works there," Rosie said quietly.